James Sheridan Knowles

True Unto Death

A drama in two acts

James Sheridan Knowles

True Unto Death
A drama in two acts

ISBN/EAN: 9783337105938

Printed in Europe, USA, Canada, Australia, Japan

Cover: Foto ©Andreas Hilbeck / pixelio.de

More available books at **www.hansebooks.com**

TRUE UNTO DEATH:

A Drama

IN TWO ACTS.

BY

SHERIDAN KNOWLES.

LONDON:

ADAMS & FRANCIS, 59, FLEET STREET ;
SIMPKIN & MARSHALL, STATIONERS' HALL COURT;
CRAMER & CO. (LIMITED) 201, REGENT STREET.

1866.

PERSONÆ.

(As produced at the Royal Strand Theatre, May 21, 1866.)

IVAN (*A Russian Nobleman*) . . . Mr. PRICE.

FREDERICK (*His Friend*) . . . . Mr. COLLETT.

ROBERT (*Landlord of the Forest Inn*) Mr. FLETCHER.

DARAN (*An Outlaw*) . . . . . Mr. PARSELLE.

ORLOFF and KARL }(*Members of His Gang*){ Mr. TURNER and Mr. THORNE.

ALEXINA (*A Young Serf*) . Miss ADA SWANBOROUGH.

CATHERINE (*Wife to Robert*) Miss MARIA SIMPSON.

The action passes at IVAN's Villa, in the suburbs of Moscow; and in the adjacent forest.

ADVERTISEMENT.

THIS Drama was written for the present proprietors by the late Mr. J. SHERIDAN KNOWLES, but has never been printed or produced till now, having remained untouched in their possession ever since it was delivered by the author. It was originally written in Three Acts, but it has been considered advisable to compress these into Two.

LONDON, *May 21st*, 1866.

TRUE UNTO DEATH.

ACT I.

SCENE I.—*Front Scene representing a room in Ivan's villa in the suburbs of Moscow.*

Enter IVAN, *in travelling costume, and* FREDERICK.

FREDERICK.

So Ivan flies the Court? resolved to roam—
What makes him go?

IVAN.

A vacant heart!

FREDERICK.

Whose heart
Is full and Ivan's vacant? Rank is his,
And wealth to wait upon it! Youth, with form
And face to use it; heart, with wit to guide it;
And spirit, spite of lets, to bear him through!
Then, with the sex we love, who rivals Ivan?
Might women's tongues talk freely as their eyes,

No maid was e'er beset as Ivan were!
In self-defence he must have ta'en a wife.

IVAN.

In self-defence who strives against himself?
Took Ivan wife, then were there end to Ivan!
For who would have this happy spirit bound
When free to roam the earth, and, loving it,
In this or that fair region to abide?
So never saw I that fair woman yet
For love of whom my heart could say, "Rest here,
Be this thy world from hence!"

FREDERICK.

Would he be wrong
Who said of Ivan, he wrong'd woman, seeing,
Desired of all, he maketh suit to none?

IVAN.

Say not desired of all, but loving all,
And yet ne'er wronging one—unlike his friend!
You love, and woo, and win, and cease to love:
So should I cease; and therefore never woo.

FREDERICK.

You love all women? You have never loved!

IVAN.

Have never loved? From youthhood until now
I dare the recreant hour would take thy part
To say it saw me not as deep in love
As ever Damon, over head and ears

Whelm'd in the magic and impetuous flood !
Deny me constant servitor to love,
And I will count you score of ruby lips,
My blushing vouchers !

FREDERICK.

Very fit they blush,
Being false witnesses !   One honest pair
Were worth them all.   Love never went beyond,
At one and the same time—nor that time brief.
I never was in love.   A miracle
To ordinary flesh and blood it is,
How heart can cleave to heart tenaciously,
Nor in the wide world find attraction else,
Yea, 'gainst persuasion of the senses even,
Known matchmakers in love.   An uncouth mien,
Fray'd skin, coarse features, harsh attunèd tongue,
Gain the love-warded heart, impregnable,
From other source to siege, of eye or ear.

IVAN.

You talk of *woman's* love !   Men love not so.
So love not you.   And yet have I a thought,
That love asks more than meets the eye and ear
In melody and beauty : So the lack
Of that's the secret of my discontent.
I have banqueted to surfeit upon smiles,
Where'er I turn that meet me : A blank cheek
For rarity were feasting.

FREDERICK.

Such a one
I could have shown you a brief month ago,
And one as fair as blank ! A serf of mine
Whom I had watch'd from budding womanhood
Unto the full unfolding of the flower,
With aim, on my own terms, to make her mine.
Thou shouldst have seen the lord entreat his serf,
The indignant serf repulse her lord—and make him
Forbear for very shame.

IVAN.

And yet thy serf ?
Resolve this riddle.

FREDERICK.

Mark ! Designing her
For my especial pleasures, early care,
By my wise forethought had its training hand
Applied to her fresh mind—a richer soil
Than my anticipations counted on ;
But by her heart surpassed, which greedily
Did of the culture of the other most
Untoward, unexpected profit make !
I saw her not from girlhood till the lapse
Of ripening years had partly done their work,
I then beheld, and wonder'd—woo'd—was spurned !
Beyond enduring piqued, I told my will
And warn'd her next we met, to know her lord !

IVAN.

And did she ?

FREDERICK.

No ; forthwith she fled without
The privacy of kin or friend, nor left
Trace that could give pursuit.

IVAN.

Give *me* that serf !
Suppose I find her ?   That most worthy serf,
Least worthy such to be.

FREDERICK.

Thou'dst hope to thrive ?

IVAN.

No ! I would act more nobly.   Heav'n ! if with props
Of wealth and rank—pure lineage—lofty kin—
Women of quality who keep fair names
Command our reverence, what should we pay
To her, who, base in stock, is virtuous ?
I'll buy thy serf from thee at any cost !

FREDERICK.

Talk not of buying.   Find her, she is thine !

IVAN.

Nay ! it must be a valid bargain though ;
We'll seal and sign, whereto you must accept
Consideration in exchange for her.

FREDERICK.

Whate'er you will.

IVAN.

It shall be worth your while :
Yourself shall name it to your full content.
We'll in and write, and have our witnesses.
(*Aside.*) At any cost to own this noble serf
Is paying cheaply for her.

FREDERICK.
I believe

I told you she was fair ?

IVAN.
Let her be so :

Her face and form are least of woman's dow'r.

Exeunt.

SCENE II.—*Set, representing a rude Hostelry seven
or eight versts from Moscow. Stairway leading to
bed room; a log fire is burning; settles, chairs and
table; guns, kitchen utensils, &c. are hung on the
walls; a spinning wheel, at the side.*

Sounds of quarrelling heard off between CATHERINE
and ROBERT. *They enter hastily at back,* ROBERT
first, and come down front.

CATHERINE.
Why, Robert, rate you me ? What if she saw
The baggage of the traveller ? No fear
He'll ever come to claim it ! Heed it not.

ROBERT.

'Twas oversight to have it there ; might cost
More than an angry word ; perchance a life!
What said she when she saw it—when you told her
The traveller was gone ?   What said she, wife?

CATHERINE.

Whate'er she might have said, did not thy wife
With ready wit forestall ?   Be sure she did !
Invoked St. Anthony, St. Nicholas,
St. Ursuline, St. Bridget, and St. Ruth,
And all their comrades i' the calendar ;
And clapp'd my hands and wrung them—made pretence
To run to the door as if to sally forth,
And then ran back again; ope'd and shut down
The window in the selfsame moment—'gan
As I would tell her errand she should go,
And stop'd in the middle on't—then clapp'd and wrung
My hands, and call'd on all the saints again !

ROBERT.

And made she no remark ?

CATHERINE.

She had perhaps,.
But that I found her occupation—sent her
In case of further oversight, to search
His chamber—call'd her back again ere well
She had sped half way—propounded other orders,.
And in the next breath countermanded them !
Then fell to fault-finding with the whole male

Creation—no such thing as bearing with them !
How but for wives and mothers and the like
They would be worse than good for nothing ! Leave
His baggage and set off no one knows whither !
And waiter, hostler, landlord standing by
And let him do it ?

ROBERT. *(Laughing.)*
Came I in for my share ?

CATHERINE.

Be sure you did ! Had you been by, good husband,
You had come in for more !

ROBERT.

I'm quite content !
Then has she no suspicion ?

CATHERINE.

None !

ROBERT.

'Tis well !
And had you thought to lead her mind astray
As to the care the honest host would take
Of the forgetful traveller's property ?

CATHERINE.

I did ! complained of lumber here and there,
How one's own property was care enough
Without the charge of other people's. How
Trouble unask'd for must make up its mind
To go without reward—how, in this world,

Though roguery still drives the briskest trade,
Still honest people must discharge their duty,
Take no account of cost, or care, or pains,
But for requital trust to Providence!

ROBERT.

This girl has brought us luck! Since she came here
'Tis bare a month, and lo! a prize already!
She has brought us luck, will bring us more; her looks
Are credit to our house.

Enter ALEXINA *unperceived at top of stair—she listens.*

CATHERINE. (*Pouting.*)
Has no one else
Good looks?

ROBERT. (*Fondling her.*)
Art jealous? If thy maid be fair,
Art thou less so? Thou 'rt for the host, good wife,
She for the guest. Thou know'st I love thee well;
And from thy smiles (thou never did'st grant more)
Make grudgingly my bait to fish for gold,
When the rich traveller that visit pays
We wish him to delay, yet not repeat.
Though not thy match, this girl thy place supplies,
And needing shelter, scarce will be in haste
To quit the roof that yields it to her. Meantime,
Our gains count double, but our cares keep pace.
The help she brings us brings with it strange eyes,
The which behoves we watch for danger, wife;
On thy account alone I shrink from it;

I heed not for myself, or what my death,
Or when the time. (*Starts*) Hark! was that not a cry
Borne from the forest? (*A faint halloa is heard off.*

CATHERINE.

Ay, methinks I catch
The winding of a bugle!

ROBERT.

Then is Karl
But good as his word. Bestir! the quarry's nigh!

ROBERT *runs off at back.* CATHERINE *looks hastily
around the room and exit;* ALEXINA *concealing
herself the while.*

Enter ALEXINA *down stairway, agitated. She comes
front.*

ALEXINA.

My fears are true! This is a house of blood!
'Twas all pretence! No traveller did depart
Ere break of day, or wherefore was not I
Forewarned to rise, as fits my place? I heard
The sound of footsteps stealing 'long the floor
At dead of night; of doors that ope'd and shut;
Of people whispering like those who do
An evil thing in dread; in caution one,
In haste another, in alarm a third;
Now speaking one by one, now all at once,
Now death-like still, as though they held their breath,
Together moving as they pass'd my door,

As if some burthen they would safe bestow,
And vanishing alike.   I am sure a house
Of blood!   The cup she gave to me was drugged!
The taste repell'd my palate.   I contriv'd
Without detection to dispose of it ;
Thus, what was meant for sleep warn'd wakefulness.
I rose too much betimes this morning, so
Disturb'd them unawares, the spoil unhid :
Whate'er betide, I quit this fearful roof—
Whither alas ! to go ? no matter, whither !
If here I bide, with murder I consort !
Yet, should I wrong them ? Innocence has paid
For worse appearances. They come: I'll prove them !

Enter ROBERT *at back, and* CATHERINE, R. *They start
on seeing* ALEXINA.

ROBERT (*aside to* CATHERINE.)
I see no sign of traveller.

CATHERINE.

Bide your time ;
Take care that she suspects not.   Why rose the girl
So soon this morning ?

ROBERT.

Better question her !

(*They come down one on each side of* ALEXINA.)

CATHERINE.
What ! girl, with idle hands ? Yet still she is
A hopeful waiting maid !—was up 'ere dawn
Though free to lie till sunrise !

ROBERT.

By her. eyes,
Of sleep no surfeit has she had—they are red, and
heavy.

ALEXINA.

Horrid dreams disturb'd my sleep !

(ROBERT *and* CATHERINE *exchange uneasy glances.*)

CATHERINE.

What didst thou dream ?

ROBERT.

Come, maiden, tell thy dream !

ALEXINA.

I dreamt last night a dream of terror wild ;
Methought a weary traveller lay asleep,
I heard the midnight murderer's cautious step
As with his weapon bared to smite his prey
He glided onwards to the victim's bed !
Strove to call for help—but all in vain :
My tongue was tied, my voice could frame no cry
Even when the gleaming knife was rais'd to strike—

ROBERT.   *(Terrified.)*
'Fore Heaven I swear——

CATHERINE.   *(Trembling.)*
And I—thou canst not say—

ALEXINA.
Nay, landlord! hostess! why so ill at ease?
'Twas but the ghostly tissue of a dream.
(Aside). I need no further proof.

ROBERT. *(Wiping his brow.)*
      Save up your dreams,
If you must dream, for others than for me.
My tender heart is such that at these tales
It leaps into my mouth; it bides there now.

CATHARINE.
I have no patience with thee, girl. About—
And set the evening meal. *(Aside to* ROBERT.*)* Don't
 be a fool!

ALEXINA *busies herself setting table. Knocking at
the door.*

ROBERT.
A summons. *(Looks out.)* As I live it is our prize!

CATHARINE. *(Running back to him.)*
Husband! You're off your guard.

ROBERT. *(Aside to* CATHARINE.*)*
      She pays no heed;
Did she suspect, she ne'er had told a dream
Like that to you and me. Observe the girl—
She dreams by day!—she never heard the knock!
Come, wife; 'twere best we let him in ourselves.
       Exeunt at back.

ALEXINA *(suddenly abandoning her listless manner).*
Had I o'erlooked the while they did the deed,
Not more were I assured the deed were done !
Whom have we now ! Pray Heaven no wealthy guest,
To tempt their foul, remorseless hands again !

(She goes to the window and looks out—becomes much
agitated.

Oh, woeful sight ! Oh woe ! when youth and grace,
With fortune's favour to emblazon them,
That ought to move our smiles, provoke our tears !
A noble guest indeed ! for such he looks—
His glorious presence flouting his attire,
Which yet shone gloriously ! No retinue ?
None but his driver ?   *(Returns down stage.*
                    Ha ! the same that brought
The guest of yesternight ! They are in league !
The carriage broken down—and for a shift,
Repair'd with cords !—So fell it out, before.
Heavens ! how they gave him hail, and smil'd him in,
As welcome had no end ! *(Goes back to window.*
                    Don't enter here !
Better the charnel house, and there the dead
To wait on thee, than this, the habitation
Of flesh and blood. Its tenants would look grim—
But here are those who welcome with grim deeds.
                    (Retires from window.
I'll warn him of his danger when alone.
                    (Exit.

Enter Ivan *at back in travelling costume followed by* Robert *bearing cloak and valise.*

ROBERT.

Broke down, my lord, you say?

IVAN.

Why, as you see,
An utter wreck—but so far fortunate
In that we are not cast on desert land.

ROBERT.

Such accidents will happen, for our roads
Are roads by courtesy—nought else. Still, my lord,
I needs must hope that wine we make ourselves,
And viands furnished from yon waving wood,
And faggots blazing on a kindly hearth,
For your mishap shall make some slight amends.

IVAN.

Good! let but the venison and the wine
Match with your faggots and I am content.

ROBERT.

You shall not have to wait!　　　(*Bustles about.*
　　　　　　　Where art thou, wife?
Ho! Alexina, Alexina—What!
The silly wench is not a-dreaming still!
I will return anon.

(*Goes out behind. Ivan sits reflectively by the fire.*)

IVAN.

Good! I can wait.
Who can she be? For what mine eyes have seen
My wonder questions as beyond belief;
A second glance accus'd the first as blind,
Not cognisant of half it looked upon!
That from its follower in turn received
Like measure of rebuke! (*Rises, looks about, then off.*
           She comes! Entrancement
Lives in her very step! What now I feel
I never felt before nor dreamed to feel.

           Enter ALEXINA *bearing a flagon.*
           IVAN. *(Taking flagon.)*
It is not meet these gentle hands should bear
A burthen, howsoever light, for me,
Nor that thou shouldst thus lowly to me minister.

ALEXINA.

Oh sir !   *(She looks about timidly.*

IVAN.

But blessed were the lot to me,
To tend thee, and fulfil thy every wish,
Preventing fancy with the ken of love !
Oh for a life of such obedience—

           ALEXINA. *(Still troubled.)*
                       Sir !

IVAN.

To do thy will for ever !

ALEXINA.

Ah!

IVAN.

Till now
I was a stranger to the fascination
Which, out of thousand women, one alone
Endows with power to bless us. I had sought it,
But at the end no nearer to it proved
Than at the setting out—I deemed it nought
And lo! when I had given it up 'tis here!

ALEXINA.

Oh mock me not!   Seek not with idle words
To tempt a simple maiden—though her heart
Beats fast on thy account.

IVAN.

What dost thou say?

ALEXINA.

Mistake me not—'tis not in wanton riot
My blood runs wildly; not for love
My pulses quicken; but I could not bear
To see thy young life ended——

IVAN.

How? my life!

ALEXINA.

Yes! Oh, sir, 'tis in fearful jeopardy!
Thou'rt in the den of murder, where to 'scape

C

Fate worse than death have I unwittingly
Till yesternight sojourned : to-night, unless
Heav'n succour thee, thou diest !

IVAN. *(Walks to and fro in thought.)*

Could I send

Tidings to the next post ?

ALEXINA.

There's none to bear them.

IVAN.

Some passing travellers may bring me aid ?

ALEXINA.

Alas, not this way lies the public track.
Who travel hither see no journey's end
Save that of life—a dread, untimely, one !

IVAN.

What's to be done ?

ALEX. *(Passionately.)*

But if you die, I'll die

Along with you ! *(Recollecting herself.*

What have I said ?

IVAN.

Enough

To make me wish to live, as ne'er I wished ! *(pause.)*
Is she who seems to order in the house,
That buxom dame, well framed, with blazing eye,
The mistress on't ?

ALEXINA.

She is.

IVAN.

The landlord's wife?

ALEXINA.

His wife.

IVAN.

I 'gin to catch a glimpse of hope!

ALEXINA.

No hope from her!—their hearts and thoughts are one.
Affinity of nature here supplies
The lack of those sweet wellings of the heart
That nourish love in others—ruth to man—
Homage to heaven ; and binds these each to each,
With such adhesion as might cast reproach
On that of holier friends.

IVAN.

He loves her then ?

ALEXINA.

Much, very much !

IVAN.

A hope ! I mark'd his eye
Twice when she pass'd him.   Where she moved, they
    went,
As in her lay the mastery which ruled
The spirits that informed them—servitors

They seemed to me, as of a royal mistress ;
All bright with beaming beauty in her presence,
All blank when she was gone !

ALEXINA.

He fondly loves her.

IVAN.

Then is the fondness of my hope the less !
I leave the house in safety.

ALEXINA.

When ?

IVAN. *(Smiling.)*

To-morrow !

Guarded by friends !

ALEXINA.

Where are they ?

IVAN.

I shall find them.
Thou would'st not stay behind me, would'st thou ?

ALEXINA.

No !

I would not stay !

IVAN.

And would'st thou go with me ?

ALEXINA. *(Diffidently.)*

I fain would go.

IVAN.

Yet not with me ?

ALEXINA.

With him
Who pledged his honour for a maiden's safety!

IVAN.

The pledge you need I give.

ALEXINA.

I'll go with thee
When and where'er thou goest.   *(They shake hands.*

IVAN.

Now be brave!
Whate'er I say or do let naught surprise thee :
Hold fear an alien to thee.   With the help,
Yea, of the self-same hands that plot my death,
Will I contrive my safety.   Hark !—a step.

ALEXINA.

The landlord comes !   To scape suspicion, bear
That for the time I flout thee, and thy wit
Freely exert in answer to my chafing.
*(ALEXINA pretends to elude the grasp of IVAN as
ROBERT and CATHERINE enter at back, carrying
fruits, &c.)*

IVAN.

What! not a kiss ? methinks you're over coy !

ALEXINA.

To say you love me !   Only catch me trust
A gay court gentleman !

ROBERT. *(Aside to* CATHERINE.*)*
    The bait has taken,
He's in the net! *(aloud.)* Heed not the saucy jade;
The truth to tell, from morn till night she dreams
Of lovers.

    CATHERINE.
  Come, girl, ease me of my load,
Then set the upper room in order meet
For such a guest.

    IVAN *(seating himself.)*
      I cry your pardon, dame,
No upper room for me! A traveller
Should keep no state if he would see the world!
Men make a face to rank, *I* would see nature's—
Therefore the common household room for me!
*(*ALEXINA *lights candles and arranges supper, then*
retires behind and watches IVAN ; CATHERINE *spins,*
and ROBERT *waits on his guests.)*
Who churlishly would wish to be alone?
(Makes a gesture of admiration towards ALEXINA.*)*
Beauty wants 'tendance of admiring eyes,
And she shall have it, far as mine can pay
The envious servitude.

    ROBERT.
    Your will is law.

    IVAN.
Host; of your maid you are free—who woos her, may;

But if I judge your watchful eye aright,
Who tries his chance against your lady's smile,
Would need to stake his life !

ROBERT.

Nay, sir ! she's free
To smile on whom she may.

IVAN.

And you are right ;
She were to pity else, and ne'er would smile,
Seeing she loves to smile on none but thee.
How long since you were married? Do you know
What marriage is ? A thousand different things !
A gain, a loss—a partnership, a breach !
A song, a dirge !—a peace, or furious war !
An airy chamber, or close prison cell !
A cushioned chair, the stocks ! a feast, a famine !
A laughing dance, a frowning funeral !
How long is 't since you married ?

ROBERT.

Come next week,
Six months.

IVAN.

Six months, and yet the honeymoon !
Why, by the dalliance of your loving eyes,
Encountering one another clear and bright,
As with the freshness of a new crowned wish—
As bees from flowers bear honey to the hives :
I should have guessed six days, before six months !

Why, you are miracles of wedded love !
Patterns, I will not say ; for if, before
Was never seen the like, how may we hope
The like again to see? (*rises.*) A boon, I pray!

ROBERT.

What is it, noble sir ?

IVAN. (*leading* CATHERINE *down* c., *and standing
between her and* ROBERT.)
Let me adopt you !

ROBERT and CATHERINE.

Oh, sir !

IVAN.

I pray you do, as an example
To wedded pairs to come !—I will not say,
We'll make the married state a perfect thing ;
But we may mend it ! Suffer me to take
The trouble of your fortune off your hands !

ROBERT and CATHERINE.

Nay, sir !

IVAN.

'Tis still the fate of modesty
To stand in its own light !

ROBERT and CATHERINE.
You are too good !

IVAN.

And if I am, be your deserts to blame,
That make me so!—I would have given the world
To have been at your wedding! But there's no loss
Which may not be made up, with proper pains!
Some day may make amends for missing that.

ROBERT.

Sure never landlord welcom'd guest so free!

CATHERINE.

Nor landlady!—so kind! so humorous!

ROBERT.

So generous!

CATHERINE.

Well favour'd too withal.
Were I a maid, my fortune were soon told!

IVAN.

The choice that is debarred, is quickly made!
What were this moment done, could it be done,
Being to be done, will take an hour of thought,
Perhaps be then no forwarder in act!
Your handsome maid, good dame, has eyes as well:
Ask her to take me!

ALEXINA.

'Tis not *eyes* that see,
It is the soul, to which they tender light;
So men the self-same thing see differently.

IVAN (*To* CATHERINE.)

Your maid is apt of wit—

CATHERINE (*Angrily.*)
More apt of tongue.
(*A knock at the door.*

CATHERINE (*Aside to* ROBERT.)

Who knocks?

ROBERT (*Aside to her.*)
'Tis Karl returned. (*Aloud*) Open the door!

(ALEXINA *opens door. Enter* KARL.

IVAN.

My pleasant charioteer!

KARL.
An honest lad, sir.

ROBERT (*Aside to* KARL, *after checking him for speaking.*)

Say, have you found our friends? and will they come?

KARL (*Aside.*)

I have; at midnight you may count upon them—

ROBERT (*Aside.*)

They will be here?

KARL (*Aside.*)
As sure as midnight comes.

ROBERT (*Aside.*)

That's sure enough!

ALEXINA (*Aside to* IVAN.)
You mark!

IVAN (*Aside to her.*)
I do! fear not,
I am prepared! (*turns to* ROBERT.) You say, by break-
fast time,
All will be ready? he can then proceed?

ROBERT.

Ay, and before, sir—

IVAN.
I have travell'd, host,
Yet never was at home at inn before.
Come hither, lad! why do you hang your head?
(*To* KARL.

ROBERT.

The boy is bashful, sir!

KARL.
I always blush
When a gentleman speaks to me!

IVAN.
I dare be sworn,
A lad as good as modest! Would you take
Service with me?

KARL.

La, sir !

IVAN.

I have a fancy
For a simple country lad ; but ne'er till now
Found one to my liking : we shall talk to-morrow.
Oh lucky overthrow, that brought me hither !
Landlord, I like your house, I like your wife,
I like your maid, I like your modest boy,
And last, nor least of all, I like yourself!
You look so thorough-going honest ! Hark you,
Would'st bear the burthen of a trifling charge ?
I like my quarters here so well, I mean
To take them up again—and shortly, too !
This box holds treasure (*lifts valise*), sorry silver, host !
A traveller of old, I had my fears
Coming this lonely road. I dreamt not, then,
To meet with friend like you. Luck doesn't come
At every hour or every turn of the road !
And, sooth, I am o'er provided ! Be my Banker
Till I return—unless I make too bold—
Will you ?

KARL.

Yes ! Sure he will, sir !

ROBERT.

Silence !

IVAN.

Nay !

Blame not the kindly, honest, modest lad,
Who errs thro' forwardness to serve your friend.
And, landlord, are you well provided, here,
'Gainst customers who love free quarters—come
And go, as list them, and ne'er call for bills ?
For, next I tax your welcome, I intend
To travel with the bulk of that in gold.

KARL.

The house is safe, sir !

ROBERT.

Silence, oaf, again !

IVAN.

Nay, a good lad, indeed ! a clever lad !
An honest lad, a modest lad, and kind—
Too kind perhaps—his only failing, that ;
Here, landlord, take my coin—I pray you do—
And hoard it surely under lock and key !

KARL.

I'll answer for him, sir !

ROBERT.   (*Pushing him to the door.*)

To bed you lout !

Nor yet o'ersleep yourself, but be astir
Betimes, to wait upon the gentleman !

(KARL exits at back.

ALEXINA. (*Aside.*)

It draws near bedtime. If to means like these
He trusts for safety he but cheats himself!
Or aims he thus to throw them off their guard?

IVAN.

Come, host; a flask and goblet! We must drink.

(ROBERT *exits* R.

I trust you are not jealous, landlady,
That I prefer your spouse to guard my dross?
The host is still the pillar of the house;
For trust, no odds I am sure, 'twixt him and you?

CATHERINE.

I take in kindness, sir, whate'er you give.
Now, would I let myself, it were not hard (*Aside.*)
To like so simple, free, and blythe a spark!

ROBERT *re-enters with a flask and goblet.*

IVAN. (*Taking the bottle and examining it.*)

Ha!—this will do!—I feel the generous wine,
Before the cork is out!—then draw it, host!
The goblet give to me—when these bright lips
Have pledg'd the wine, I'll teach you how to drink.
Have measure of a right good thirsty soul!

ALEXINA.

(*Aside to* IVAN *having watched the looks of* ROBERT *and*
CATHERINE *who betray some anxiety.*)

The wine is drugged.

IVAN. (*Aside to her.*)
　　　I'll prove if it be so—
Host, the first cup is yours ! 　　　　(*To* ROBERT.

ROBERT. (*Refusing.*)
　　　　By your favour, sir !

IVAN.
Nay, no excuse, but drink !

CATHERINE. (*Aside to* ROBERT.)
　　　　Pretend to drink !
(ROBERT *barely puts the cup to his lip, and removes*
　it.)

IVAN.
Sip with a toper, host ! 　Why, drink the draughts :
Off with it, till no tell-tale drop be left
To trickle to the brim : I wait the cup.

CATHERINE. (*Aside to* ROBERT.)
Say that the flask is bad—the rest are honest.
For a deep draught will drug to sleep as well,
And he's the spark to take one !

IVAN. (*Aside to* ALEXINA.)
　　　　They're at fault.

ALEXINA. (*Aside to him.*)
He will not drink ! 　I knew the wine was drugg'd !

ROBERT.
What's this ?
　　(*Pretends to dislike the wine and spits it out.*

CATHERINE.

Good wine? *(smells bottle)* a damaged flask?
How came we by it?

IVAN. *(Smiling furtively.)*

Fetch another, host;
And leave this here. No man shall drink bad wine
In house of friend of mine, while I can help,
So, there go flask and all!—I'll pay the cost.

(Flings it into the fire.

ROBERT.

I'm very sorry, sir—

IVAN.

I'm very glad!
Another sample of a better sort!

(ROBERT goes out, R.
I'll empty every flask till one shall fit,
And fill your cellar should I run it out.

(Re-enter ROBERT with another bottle.
Now draw, and fill, and drink! That flask is good:
I test the draught by looking in your eye,
Bright spokesman of your palate! Fill again!
Hostess, the richest wine wants flavour which
The lip of woman gives it!

CATHERINE. *(Drinking.)*

Health and fortune, Sir!

IVAN.

Health will suffice—no fortune good as health!

Now, maiden, yours the cup! and after you
       (Passes it to ALEXINA.*)*

It comes to me; and so our lips may meet
Without offence, join'd by the blushing cup.
That saves your cheeks, but gives a glow to mine
Who know I meet the kiss you thought not of!
Health to thee, maiden—body's health—and health
Far richer of the heart—such blessed ground
Should grow no wish or hope to mourn a blight.
        (Drinks.)

ROBERT.

Sooth, Sir, I would not be an anchorite,
To pass an hour with you; it would go hard
But I should break my vows!

IVAN. *(Affecting partial intoxication.)*

      'Tis time to sleep!
The hour, or else the cup, persuades me so!
Landlord, to bed!

ROBERT. *(Taking up candles.)*

    I'll show you to your room!

IVAN.

I'faith, you shall not, host!—I never yet
Took groom to light me thither! Tripping feet
Of maid, or housewife, do that office best.
I mean all honestly! What piping page
Could say " good night " as this sweet maiden can,

Leaving a seraph's blessing in mine ear,
To wile me to my rest? Give *her* the lights!
Though, as a stranger's trust is just as far
As keeps him well in sight, your gentle dame
Shall e'en one candle bear, for company.

(Takes one of the lights from ALEXINA, *to whom the
landlord had given both, and presents it to* CATHE-
RINE.

But if you will, go fetch a flash of wine,
Your richest, rarest, for a stirrup cup
Before I plunge into the land of dreams.
I go to bed in state! Ladies lead on.

*(*CATHERINE *and* ALEXINA *ascend stairs;* IVAN *follows,
but turns round and looks fixedly with a smile at*
ROBERT, *who takes down the cellar keys, and stands
perplexed below. The scene shuts in.*

SCENE III.—*The Inn Yard (Front Scene). Lights
down.*

Enter ROBERT, *from house bearing lanthorn. Enter
KARL—they meet.*

ROBERT.

You felt it too?

KARL.
Yes! treasure by the weight.

ROBERT.

Men travel not with iron or with lead,
He said that it was silver—

KARL.

Thanks to me!
Not in all Russia is postilion found
Could so contrive a dexterous break down,
That what was done of thought, seemed accident!
I knew my ground, and, at the point, my steed
With all my will, against my will, set off!
Now for my skill : to urge, yet seem to check,
To chide with thong, yet mean encouragement;
And with the very reins that hold him in,
To give him hint he had my leave to go!
The bank was now in sight—that friend in need—
The which behoved me shun, concerned we meet.
And would I meet it ?   No ! Though I should twist
The head off the carrion ! How I strained
By thong and rein, by knee and spur, the wheel
Should clear the bank a mile ! In the next moment
We charg'd it ! Traveller, postilion, carriage,
And carrion, in a twink were overthrown.

ROBERT. (*Giving money.*)
There for thy merits—one, two, three, four, five,
The sum I promised thee.

KARL.

A goodly sum !

D 2

Yet would not pay the setting of a bone,
Chanced I to break one. Surgeon's charges bleed
Much better than their lancets.

ROBERT.
Thou art free
From both—Give thanks !

KARL.
A goodly gift !
A man's neck is worth something. Though I ran
The risk of breaking mine—I am sure I did!
I would not be a traitor : no not for all
The traveller's box contains. I am o' the spirit
That scorns a bribe. The traveller's a great man.
He is rich—he will be missed, and search be made;
Rewards will be proclaimed for clue to him.
Who'll give it them ? Will Karl ? Give Karl the
    knout,
He would not give it them ! But then has Karl
A conscience, and his conscience likes fair play.
" Come, Karl," it says to him, " tell the secret,
Thou'rt offered fifty ducats ! What gottest thou
For keeping it ? As much ?" No, conscience! " Half ?"
Nor yet the half, dear conscience ; "Half of that ?"
Nor that ! " Ten ducats, certainly !" Take five
Away ! " Five ducats only ! Is that fair ?"
There is a poser. But is Karl the lad
That's lightly left without a word to say ?

Not he! So thus he answers conscience :—"That
Is my affair!   A bargain is a bargain !
Though 'twere the half of five, I am content ;
Halve that again, again I am content ;
Say 'twere one ducat only, and what then ;
Money to scrubs !   Karl is a lad of honour !

ROBERT.

Thou got'st what thou did'st ask !   Say that to conscience.

KARL.

So have I said to her a thousand times :
But conscience hath a very woman's tongue,
A miracle it is to silence her.
Though, had I asked thee twice the sum, no word
Had she been left to say.

ROBERT.
You're sure of that ?

KARL.

Sure ?   Certain, positive, convinc'd, content.
Nay ! conscience after all will list to reason—

ROBERT.

Yet yours methinks is but a stubborn one !

KARL.

Very ! will heed at times no will but's own ;

When in the humour 'tis to run away,
Turn it to right or left, you have a horse
With the bit between his teeth !

ROBERT.

     Five ducats more
Would go, methinks, but very little way
To put thy conscience upon terms with thee ?

KARL.

Nay ! a great way ! Already she comes round
At but the thought !

ROBERT.

    Then the reality
Would reconcile her quite ?

KARL.

     Quite ? Perfectly :
Wholly, entirely, altogether, all !

ROBERT. (*Giving more money.*)
There are five ducats, then ; and one to boot,
And hark ye, Karl—If that should come to pass
Which thou surmisedst now, give timely note ;
And I will pay for silence twice as much
As they for speech to keep thy conscience quiet.

KARL.

If honesty, as men say, oft goes bare

And sparely feeds, at other times it thrives;
And of such is the present.   It is well.

ROBERT.

And now away!—The while I fetch the wine
Shall be our traveller's viaticum.

> (KARL *goes off* R., ROBERT L.   *Change-*

SCENE IV.—*A Bed Chamber in the Inn.   Bed,*
table, chairs, etc.—door in flat.

Enter CATHERINE *and* ALEXINA *lighting* IVAN.

IVAN.

Set down the lights, but leave not yet the room,
I fain would yet enjoy your sight, fair maid,
And yours, sweet Hostess, ere I fall to sleep.

CATHERINE.

It draws near midnight.   (*Makes as if to go-*

IVAN (*restraining her*).
> Nay, you shall remain.

CATHERINE (*Aside*).

Pity, he is so frank and generous!

IVAN.

Hostess, I pray be seated   .   (*Offers chair-*

CATHERINE.

Nay, good sir.

IVAN.

I pray you do.   You are not in the room
Unless you sit.   The while you stand you go !
(*Landlady sits.   Ivan 'converses with her; Alexina
comes.*

ALEXINA (*Aside*).

What can he purpose ?   Playfulness is slight
To cope with fate so dread as threatens him.
His smiles are terror to me—make me feel
As watching one at gambols on a cliff.
And yet whene'er his eye encounters mine,
Its steady glance wakes confidence again.

IVAN (*Opening a traveller's desk*).

Hostess, a traveller at times may be
A lonely man ! when he lacks company
He finds it here.   (*Prepares to write.*
                    Your pardon while I write :
A friend, at the next station, looks for me,
And I would send him word of my mischance
By line, the which, I doubt not, my good host
Will, long ere morning, bear.   (*Writes.*

CATHERINE (*Aside*).

                    And if he should—
I scarcely should regret; but small the hope !

ALEXINA (*Aside*).

And trusts he for his rescue but to that !
Oh, woe is me ! if that's his only help
I tremble for him ! Yet how calm he looks !
What cheer of heart in all he says and docs !
Fate cannot look at him, and be his foe !
His face might turn hostility to love.

IVAN (*Folding and directing a paper*).

Thus may a traveller find company :
By calling round him his own ready thoughts
To talk with him, and make the hour pass lightly !
But travellers may want friends, and friends are things
That are not found as soon as company——
That deal in acts, not words—or words that turn
Upon the word to acts—Though, take my word,
The tongueless friend's not farthest from the best !
Here is a brace of such !

(*Opens a drawer in the desk, and takes out a brace
of pistols. CATHERINE draws back.*

                      Nay ! start not, host,
I never trifle with a friend in need
To ask his help, ere 'tis required in earnest.
But keep your seat ! 'Tis all the boon I ask——
No weapon that I wield bears harm for you ;
You fear not, gentle maid ?   (*To* ALEXINA.

ALEXINA.

Not for myself.

IVAN.

Not fearing that, all other fear put by !
Ha ! landlord !

[ROBERT *enters at back with flask, &c.*

ROBERT.

Here, sir !

IVAN.

(*Presenting pistol—Hostess starts up.*
Your seat resume !
(*Hostess sits again.*

ROBERT.

What mean you ?

IVAN.

If you will, a jest, a quip,
The drowsy night to cheat of half its pow'r,
And make our next acquaintance closer still.

(ROBERT *advances.*

No nearer, host ! (*Presenting.*) By heav'n, fall
  back again. (ROBERT *retires.*
Yet further. (ROBERT *retires again.*

Now you know your proper place ;
See that you keep it !

ALEXINA. (*Aside*).

Such command he looks
As neither stop nor question deigns consult :
And still I tremble !

IVAN.　(*To* ALEXINA).

　　　　　　　　Gentle maiden, raise
The flask and flagon with thy graceful hand ;
Your touch the draught will richer make, and give
A wealth its vintage never could bestow.
Now fill the cup, and dare the beaded tide
To kiss a lip, so sweet and full as thine !
And wish me, lady, as your knight forlorn,
Good night and pleasant dreams.　　　(*Laughing.*
　　　　　　　Heav'n save the mark !

ALEXINA (*Filling the cup and kissing it*).
I wish thee safe good night and bright good morn !

IVAN.

Whom best you love—why, pass the cup to him !
　　　　(ALEXINA *hesitates—presents the cup to* IVAN.
I taste your lip, and not the brimming tide. (*Drinks.*
The hostess !
(ALEXINA *gives* CATHERINE *the cup.　She merely
　touches it with her lips, and returns it angrily*).
　　　　　Now the host !—but no ! a moment stay—
To slight my hostess' lip were somewhat bold.
Health, and good night, my host !　　　(*Drinks.*
　　　　　Good host, good night !

ROBERT.
I mean my wife to come　　(*Makes as if for his wife*).

IVAN (*threatening* CATHERINE *with pistol*).

> Mean what you please ;
But, with your leave, as doubtless you've the right,
I mean both maid and wife to stay !

ROBERT (*Moving*).

> 'Sdeath, sir.

IVAN (*Presenting*).

Beware, sir !—Mark me well, good landlord mine,
I know my fate ! and will not bleed for thee !
Your wife, as hostage, here shall I detain,
Your maid her guard, so jealous love may sleep !

> *Takes letter from table.*

This missive wants a speedy escort—see
'Tis here by dawn !—and then your neck is safe.
Your wife released—your villain secret kept ;
But, at a sign that warrants slightest fear,
A finger on the latch, the faintest sound
Without the door, you seal her instant death !
And though one arm 'gainst hundreds I oppose,
Nor she nor I shall fall alone !   Say, then,
You catch my meaning, host ?

ROBERT (*Gloomily*).

> I do. Good night! (*going.*

CATHERINE.

Good night !   We go with you ? (*To* ROBERT.)

IVAN (*Threatening with pistols*).

> Landlord, beware!

ROBERT (*Motioning* CATHERINE *to stay*).
His highness wills you bear him company;
An honoured guest, you know, should have his way;
Mayhap he's troubled with the megrims; sprites,
Spectres, hobgoblins, come o' nights, you see,
Whenever the hired beds of stranger-folks
He presses; so to sleep he dreads to pass;
And therefore asks, sans ceremony, wife,
To have you within call.

CATHERINE (*Violently*).

> I shall not stay!

ALEXINA.
Nay, mistress, why? No ill he means us!

ROBERT (*To* CATHERINE).

> Stay!

IVAN.

She must indeed!

CATHERINE.
I'd know the reason.

IVAN.

> Know

The reason? Oh, woman, thou know'st it well!

CATHERINE (*After a pause*).

I'll stay!

IVAN.

'Tis well! Good night, my host! (*To* ROBERT.

ROBERT.

        I go—

Spare us! your pleasure shall be done by dawn.

ROBERT *goes to door and turns a lingering look on his wife.* IVAN *still holds his pistols pointed—* ALEXINA *silently thanks Heaven for the interposition.*

END OF FIRST ACT.

ACT II.

SCENE I.—*A Room in* IVAN'S *Villa* (*Front Scene*).

Enter IVAN *and* FREDERICK.

IVAN.

Well, Frederick, any word of her?

FREDERICK.

                         Not yet.
Suburbs and city have we searched in vain.
But why this yearning wish to find the maid?
Thou know'st thou wouldst abhor to do her wrong;
Why wish her back again?

IVAN.

                        To right myself
In her esteem!   Gain pardon for a wrong
I did her; and, as far as in me lies,
Requiting her for life preserved to me,
Her life preserve against mishaps, assaults;
Then with an honest blessing bid her go,
And ne'er behold her more!

FREDERICK (*Laughing*).
                              If as thou think'st
She loves thee !

IVAN.
            If ?   Good Frederick ! list to that
I would not tell before.   When, as required,
My escort came, and straight I rose to go,
Her face, till then all flush'd with watching, turn'd
The hue to match a shroud ; and so remain'd
Until as from a death-trance waking her
With summons to my side, my voice dissolv'd
The spell, and made her move, a form of life
With new infusion glowing !   Once to mine
Her eye she lifted !   'Twas one only look !
But with that look she gave me all her soul !

FREDERICK.
And was that all ?

IVAN.
                Once woman tells her love
She does not quickly end but tells it on.
Long, Frederick, after we forget the theme.
Now, wilt thou listen soberly ?

FREDERICK (*Yawning*).
                              Go on.

IVAN.
My lips all mute (for what were speech to empt

A heart o'ercharged as mine with gratitude?)
I sat with eyes that strain'd their might to heav'n,
And what did she? Thank heav'n too? Ay! but how?
With tears, with sobs, words inarticulate
Except to love's own ear, which told me plain
The ample tribute all was meant for me!

FREDERICK (*flippantly*).
And took you not advantage of that hour?

IVAN.
For what?

FREDERICK.
To dally with her.

IVAN.
                  While the glow
Of Heaven's own hand, in mercy reach'd to save,
Was fresh upon me! And of all with her
Its warning angel that admonished me
What need I stood in of its help! No no!
Had I,—the spirit that has pass'd in mercy
I had deserv'd to turn on me in vengeance! (*Crosses.*

FREDERICK.
Didst thou not wonder, when, her story told,
She proved the serf I had resigned to thee?

E

IVAN.

I did, and trembled, Frederick, for myself;
To have my wish within my power, yet lack
Men's warrant to enjoy it righteously;
And have no other option, but foregoing it,
Or wearing it despoiled of ruth and honour!

FREDERICK.

And wherefore did she fly thee?

IVAN.

                    Through my fault!
I dared but breath a wish 'twas a shame to harbour;
Drooping and mute the wounded girl withdrew.
I would have call'd her back but pride prevail'd,
Reflection, back'd by love, turn'd pride to shame,
I vow'd to make amends next time we met,
Though not to the amount her merits claim'd;
(I lack'd the courage to be true to love!)
But, fatal pause! We parted not to meet.
She fled the house that hour—with her my peace!

FREDERICK (*warmly*).

Let her be mine again!

IVAN.

                  Not though a kingdom
Were thine to buy her with, and I in bondage!
I would consume with thraldom day by day
Ere see that treasure in another's hoarding.

FREDERICK.

Such hoarding, whether seen by thee or not,
Is sure to come—Heaven sends its gifts that men
Should use them! Wilt not thou, another will!

IVAN.

Frederick, there's writhing in the likelihood!
What in the proof then? Madness! Find her for me,
For till she's found I cannot think or act.
Why playest thou the niggard, wayward fortune,
When nature is most lavish of her gifts?

Exeunt.

SCENE II.—*Set. A wood close to* IVAN's *Villa in the suburbs of Moscow. Time, after Sunset. Practicable winding path behind, descending amongst shrub-grown rocks; rustic bridge, with little rill; borders cut foliage; a fallen tree.*

ORLOFF *discovered sitting on tree, with his gun by his side.* KARL, *still dressed as Postilion, is standing draining a hunting flask which* ORLOFF *has handed him.*

ORLOFF.

Nay, tell us, Karl, how fell it out, good lad?

KARL.

The quarrel?—Marry, anger led to it.

ORLOFF.

A not unlikely cause!   Anger will lead
To a quarrel.   But what led to anger, Karl?

KARL.

A difference.

ORLOFF.

Ay! now you are coming to it!
What made the difference?

KARL.

A difficulty.

ORLOFF.

Closer and closer!   Now, the difficulty?

KARL.

How to agree.

ORLOFF.

And what the question vex'd
Of the agreement, touching which the difficulty;
Which difficulty led to difference,
And so on to a quarrel?

KARL.

What the question
Of agreement?   None!   Said I not to thee plainly,
How they could not agree.   (*Aside.*) 'Twould never do
To come from the town, nor show you had been there.

ORLOFF. (*Rising and crossing.*)
But touching what ?
What could they not agree on ?

KARL.

What could they not agree on ? So !—Oho !
Why, now, I understand you ! You speak plain !
That's coming to the point ! Whene'er you ask
A question, as you hope to get an answer,
Come to the point !—So, now your answer ! See
The use of coming to the point ! You have
Your answer.

ORLOFF.

How ! this tells me nothing, Karl !

KARL.

Why, nothing can I tell you !

ORLOFF. (*Aside.*)
What a fool
The town has made of him ! We shall be quits
Before we part, though ! He shall tell me that
I know as well as he. (*Aloud.*) A strange adventure
Was that about the girl——

KARL.
That saved the life of Daran ?

ORLOFF.
How it came to pass I know not.

KARL.

Why, thus it came to pass.   Daran had died,
But that saved his life.

ORLOFF.

'Twas well for Daran !

KARL.

That's as it proves, Daran may come to the knout.
Now death is death ! and yet is not one death
Another death !   Stabbing is not the same
As shooting !   Would you say a strangled man
Was drown'd ?   The end is one, the means are many,
And there the difference lies !   What kind of death
Would you like best to die?

ORLOFF.

Like best ?

KARL.

Come, come !
'Tis clear there is a difference, and where
A difference is a choice is sure to be,
And where a choice of course a preference.
Which of these deaths would you prefer to die?

ORLOFF.

None ?

KARL.

You amaze me !   Were I in the strait,
And had my choice, my mind would be made up
In a moment !

ORLOFF.

Which way, then, would you prefer ?

KARL.

Which way ?   Which way ?—I'll tell another time ;
There is no hurry now.   One thing is clear—
No death like the knout !   Daran was near it once,
Whence sprung the brawl with Robert.

ORLOFF.   (*Aside.*)

Now then comes
At last the story !—I shall seem to pay
No heed to it, so shall I hear it through !   (*Walks up
and down.*)

KARL.

Will you listen, Orloff ?

ORLOFF.

Yes, if you make haste !

KARL.

When was I slow ?—When did I not make haste ?
Come to the point at once, when 'twas my time ?

ORLOFF.   (*Aside.*)

You take your time !

KARL.

Count Ivan, as you know—

ORLOFF.

And if I know, why do you tell it me ?

KARL.

Must everything be new ?   Can naught be told
Save what is new ?   Take you the rarest tale
That ever wonder cried " Heaven save us " at,
There shall be something old !   Be thankful, then,
Take old and new together, or take nought !
Count Ivan, as you know, sav'd Daran's life.

ORLOFF.

Well, have you done ?

KARL.

Done ? here's a man for a story
He does not know the end from the beginning !

ORLOFF.

Why, is there more to hear ?

KARL.

More !   Say'st thou, more ?
'Twere a fine story, which three words could tell !
A pretty kind of story.

ORLOFF.

'Twould be sweet,
According to the adage—" short and sweet ! "
But to the end, for I'm in haste !   (*Catches gun up.*)

KARL.   (*Taking hold of his wrist.*)
You'll wait
For the middle, won't you ?

ORLOFF.

Yes, so you take care
Not to stick in the middle ! (*Replaces gun.*)

KARL.

Stick ? Not I—
I ne'er left off in tale I once began,
While word remain'd to tell !—Robert has plann'd
The death of the Count to-night. This Daran knows,
And hence the breach. He would not have him die
Who saved him from the knout. A near escape
Had Daran, without knife, when Robert drew ;
When in the thicket couch'd up springs a youth,
And holds a sword to him ! This turns the odds
But Daran spares the man had murder'd him, and
    lets him go.

ORLOFF. (*Aside.*)
I know the rest !—Good bye (*makes as if to go.*)

KARL. (*Stopping him*).
Nay, half the tale's to tell ! You'll hear the whole ?
The strippling swoon'd soon as he gave the sword,
And—

. ORLOFF.
Lay as he were dead !—(*going.*)

KARL. (*Holding him back.*)
Stone dead !—whereon—

ORLOFF.

They bore him to the brook, and he reviv'd !

> (*taking another step.*

KARL.

After a time—a long time—during which—

ORLOFF.

Loosening his doublet—(*Still retreating.*)

KARL.

> Yes, to give him—

ORLOFF.

> Air,

KARL.

They found the stripling was—

ORLOFF.

> A girl !

KARL.

> Disguised !

ORLOFF. (*Returning and resting on his gun.*)
Of course ! How else had she for stripling pass'd ?

KARL.

The man who mars a tale would cut a throat !
At least, should have his own cut. Thou knows't all ?
Nought is thy all ! Who was the girl ? Tell that !

ORLOFF.

Nay, tell thou that—I know not!

KARL.

Tell thyself!

When thou would'st borrow, brag not of a purse,
Or he that's woo'd to lend may chance to mock!
Who was the girl? I know!

ORLOFF.

I care not!

KARL.

Right!

Be of the fox's mind! Say, 'tis not worth
The having! Guess you why he said the grapes
Were sour? Because they hung above his reach?
No!—but because he knew the grapes were sweet
Could he but crunch them!

ORLOFF.

Know I not the rest as well as thou!

KARL.

How she was chambermaid to the inn which Robert
kept?

ORLOFF.

Yea, more!

KARL.

What; How

She betray'd him to Count Ivan?

ORLOFF.

More than that!

KARL.

What! How the Count escaped?

ORLOFF.

More still.

KARL.

And took—

Orloff, what took the Count along with him?

ORLOFF.

Thou wantest me to tell! Thou dost not know,
Thy looks betray thee! Shall I tell thee, Karl?
Why, then, he took——

KARL.

The maid along with him.
I hope I know the rest of the story now.

ORLOFF.

Ay, well as I that knew not word before!
Nay, spare your choler! 'Tis my turn to-day;
It may be yours to-morrow! Hands, good Karl!
And welcome to the baudit's haunt again!
'Twas well you broke with Robert!

KARL.

For my skin!
I have a conscience! It were reasonable

To run a light risk for a heavy gain.
But when the gain and risk change scales, I stop—
Because I have a conscience.   Robert wants
Revenge—I don't !   He cares not for his life—
I do for mine !   He swears the Count shall die—
I never swear to anything except
I know 'twill come to pass, because I have
A conscience.   Orloff, ever have a conscience !

ORLOFF.

The town, I see, has taught you something, Karl !
Now, wherein differ those who dwell in towns
From us ?

KARL.

          In this—they have no consciences ;
But I must leave thy pleasant company,
Or make my bed with thee upon the grass,
Finding fast closed the city gates.

ORLOFF.

                              By fortune
You have not far to go . I wish myself
'Twere further—that for safety's sake, good Karl !
But Daran wills, and Orloff must.   And hist,
By that same token here he comes.   (*Whistle heard.*

KARL.

                         And I
By that same token vanish !   (*Exit hurriedly.*

ORLOFF. *(Looking after him.)*

Knave and fool
Dispute dominion in his coward soul! *(Looks behind.)*
Ha! she is with him, and in earnest converse.
Perchance I'm one too many. So I go. *(Exit.*

Enter down winding path the outlaw DARAN *with*
ALEXINA *dressed in male attire and leaning on him;*
they come down, and he seats her gently on the fallen
tree.

DARAN.

Thy tale is strange!   To love, and yet forego,
Thyself of state so lowly—his so high!
Riches and rank bow virtue of themselves :
Yet here, tho' back'd by love, like feathers weigh!
'Tis very strange!   Thou surely art belov'd
Of Him who round and round us sends the sun
To cheer the world, and no distinction makes,
But gives to king and robber share alike!
I am a rude, unletter'd man, and yet
I know what goodness is—could love it, too!
Thou sav'dst my life!

ALEXINA.

It cost me nothing.

DARAN.

No!
But might have cost thee much, had he prevail'd,
By whom 'twas jeopardised!   I say again,

And contradict me not, for I am rash,
Else had I never in such peril stood—
Thou savedst my life !—and nothing in return
Do I for thee ? (*Musing.*)

ALEXINA.

If I should name a thing——

DARAN.

Name it

ALEXINA. (*Essaying to kneel.*)
Protect the life of him I love !

DARAN. (*Preventing her.*)
You know 'tis threatened then ?

ALEXINA.
You know it too !   My fears then warn'd me rightly.

DARAN.
If they did, you know he dies to-night.

ALEXINA.

Oh heav'n !

DARAN.
Therefore to yonder villa, which beneath the walls
Of the grey city flickers like a dream,
Goes he this very night, from whom you saved me.

ALEXINA.

Oh, sir !

DARAN.

Inevitable is the blow !
And when, reclined upon his couch, he waits
For sleep he meets with death !

ALEXINA.

To-night ?

DARAN.

To-night !

ALEXINA.

Ah me !

DARAN.

And though I owe
A heavy debt to him, for from the knout
He sav'd me once——

ALEXINA.

Yes, yes !

DARAN.

Yet must I say,
Repaying thee with evil—(for, to the act
The will is as the spirit to the body—
The life on't—without which you have a corse
That can't avail a wagging finger's worth)—
Repaying thee in such wise, naught he meets
But his deserts !—I would not turn my hand
To save him !

ALEXINA. (*Rising and crossing.*)
  I would give my hand itself
And limb on limb : yea—everything, except
What I must render, far as in me lies,
Perfect again to heaven !

   DARAN. (*Half aside, to himself.*)
    She sav'd my life !

    ALEXINA.

Think of thy debt to him ; or what thou say'st
Thou owest me make huge as e'er thou wilt,
I'll throw it into his account, so that
Thou payest. Yea, will from thy creditor
Into thy debtor turn, who day by day
Shall weary Heav'n for blessing to repay thee !

   DARAN. (*Aside.*)
How truthfully her gentle nature works
It were the way !

    ALEXINA.
  Oh, sir, the Count is good !
His generosity rebukes his love ;
Which only fail'd, to wish thing it did !
Which when he breath'd, his tongue itself condemn'd,
That flatter'd more than spoke—while glanc'd aside
His eye, ashamed to countenance the act,
And on his cheek his better nature glow'd.

          F

DARAN. (*Aside.*)

He is the man she paints.   It were the way !

ALEXINA.

And, oh, sir, what impediments of ruth
And reason will not love, in men, o'erleap ?
And how the world o'erlooks its trespassers ?
Half which, and more, lay to the world's account,
That gives its countenance against its lips.
O ! help him, sir, or show to me the way,
And see if 'tis not taken, soon as known !

DARAN.

My heart inclines to save him : let me think.

ALEXINA.

Do so : and I will lift my heart the while
To Heaven to guide thy thoughts !

DARAN.

'Tis hard
To lay one's own life for another down,
Tho' cherish'd ne'er so dearly.

ALEXINA.

——Yes, 'tis hard ;
But those methinks I know would do as much.

DARAN.

Then, to be murder'd in cold blood !

ALEXINA.

'Tis but
The thought ! The thing's the same !

DARAN.

I spoke of *him*.

ALEXINA.

The Count—Oh, Heav'n ! my blood is all congeal'd.

DARAN.

One chance is left him. Could we find
One that would take his place—

ALEXINA.

What ! sleep alone
To-night in his bed ?

DARAN.

—And there abide the blow
That's meant for him. For there must be a victim ;
Blood must be shed, that safety be procured !
To baulk the assassin with an empty couch
Were but to place the date of Ivan's death
Beneath another moon. (*Pause*) But how contrive it—.

ALEXINA.

Ay—how ? the rest is nothing !

DARAN.

Nothing ! What !
Nothing to find a friend to die for us ?

ALEXINA.

Find thou the way, and I shall find the friend.

DARAN.

Behoves his object be concealed :

ALEXINA.

Of course—
The Count of his own life would make a wreck,
Ere friends he loves should founder for its sake !

DARAN.

Nay, for this cause besides : I were foresworn,
If thro' my measures warning reach'd the Count
Or any of his household ; yet behoves
That he who saves him see him.

ALEXINA.

See him ! What—
And he discover'd ?

DARAN.

Not were he disguised.

ALEXINA.

(*Recollecting her own disguise.*) (*Aside.*)
Good ! Good ! Now, Fortune, makest thou amends
For all bad turns gone by ! (*Aloud.*) But, at a word,
The well-known voice betrays. Ah ! there again
Is danger !

DARAN.

Yes ; but not if he were mute
As he were deaf and dumb ?

ALEXINA.

I see the way !
I bear a letter from you to the Count,
In which—but more of this anon—you hint
That what in love he seeketh he shall find :
That here by leafy margent of the wood
You wait his instant coming.   Without doubt
He'll come all eagerly ; and in his haste
Forget the humble messenger.

DARAN.

And then ?

ALEXINA.

Oh trust me !   Ne'er was labyrinth yet
Too intricate for woman, so the core
But held the thing she loved !   How then can I,
Loving as I do, chance to fail in quest
Of that sweet death that seals my love for him ?
Ah ! all's before me !   I shall set it down,
And you, anon, shall sign what I indite.
Cans't write ?

DARAN.

Why, yes ; the Count well knows my hand.

ALEXINA.

He knows your hand ?   All's right—all's clear—all's
  done.

(*Takes out tablets, kneels before the tree and writes*

DARAN (*Aside*).

Oh earnest love ! Oh most ingenious love !
Quick'ning her wits to save her lover's life
By shipwreck of her own.—Oh, truthful maid !
The purpose snatching up before me, which
I all along kept eye on, and pursued.
And, if thou run'st thy bark upon this beach,
Thoul't find a haven where thou see'st a grave !

ALEXINA. ¨¯(*Rising, and reading from paper.*)
Here it is :
" I have tidings for thee—of the maid who flies,
Who shuns thy suit and yet would give thee all.
An arrow's flight beyond thy garden rim
I wait thee in the precincts of the forest.
Naught knows my messenger—question him not ;
He's deaf and dumb ; nor tarry to conjecture,
But on the instant come ! "

DARAN.
'Tis well.

ALEXINA.
Now sign,
And let me quick begone.   To-night, you said,
And lo ! the night is here.   Sign quick—I pray.

(DARAN *signs and gives her the letter—she puts it in*
her breast. ALEXINA *is about to go when* DARAN
restrains her, and takes her hand.

DARAN.

So eager, too! Prompt will falls soon to work!
Stay!—let me read your hand before you go!

ALEXINA. (*Withdrawing her hand.*)
Nay! for my fate is told, so fare thee well!

[*Waves him adieu and Exits.*

DARAN. (*Looking after her.*)
And now for Ivan—on his heart's your life—
For if he's base, 'tis better you should die.
Ha! footsteps! peasants, doubtless, for the town.
DARAN *retires up behind, and conceals himself behind
tree. Enter* ROBERT, CATHERINE, *and others,
disguised in mantles. They hesitate as to their
path, and come down.*

CATHERINE.

Robert!

ROBERT.

How, wife?

CATHERINE.

Thou hast not called me " Kate "
Since that unlucky night.

ROBERT.

I am sour'd! 'Tis hard
To lose the game, yet hold it in our hand
But for my love of thee, the traveller,
Booty, and all were safe. Go back, I say!

CATHERINE.

No !—for my heart misgives ! Your enterprise
Will fail ! .

ROBERT.
How, Kat ?

CATHERINE.
Ay, that's the word ; Go on !
Do what thou wilt, so still thou call'st me so !

ROBERT.
Well, Kate, why should we fail ? I know the lair
Wherein this antler crouches, know the time
To take him there, and how to cheat the wind.
And shall I lose him ? No! my plan is sure.
His walls are paper ; treasures they enclose :
These shall be ours, and with them, worth them all,
Revenge! Go back and sleep, sweet Kate, till morn
Wakes thee with tidings brighter than the sun.

CATHERINE.
I'll not go back—

ROBERT.
—Thou wilt not ? Then, come on !
He baffled me before thy face, my Kate ;
Made gyves for me of thy sweet looks, and laugh'd
To see me bound with my own heart-strings !—Kate, .
I have sworn to be reveng'd ! Then, come along ;

And, for requital see me keep my oath.
He baffled me :—and let him baffle yet,
I tell thee I will hunt him to the death.
But now let's seek the trail again.   Too nigh
Our bourne, to tread the open forest path,
We'll plunge into the shrouding waste of verdure,
The velvet moss will not repeat our steps.
Nor moon-beam play the spy !

CATHERINE.

Husband, lead on !

*They exeunt cautiously.   DARAN comes down stage
and surveys them disappearing.*

DARAN.

So soon ! so nigh ! I would the Count were come.

[*Retires up and looks off.*

Ha! no shadow that of tree or rock.   It moves,
'Tis he ! but not alone.   Yonder they glide !
Does he suspect my faith ?   I soon shall know.

[*Retires up ascending path—Scene closes in.*

SCENE III.—*Another part of the Forest.   Lights
down.   Front Cloth.*

*Enter IVAN and FREDERICK, cloaked.   IVAN strives to
read a letter by the moonlight.*

FREDERICK.

And pay you trust to warrant slight as this
Signed by an outlaw ?

IVAN.

Ah, the desperate
Are prodigal of trust ! They grasp at shadows,
Yet know they melt : though here, or I mistake,
Is that which baffles fading ! Not more strange
The vanish'd maiden hereby should be found,
Than that her loss of Daran should be known.
The knowledge vouches for the remedy.
Frederick, I trust in Daran ! Had you seen
His messenger !—so had you said might look
A seraph, took he on him form of earth,
To do some merciful behest of heaven.

FREDERICK.

And Daran promises to-night to meet you here?

IVAN.

Hark ! is't a step ?

DARAN (*without.*)
Ho ! trav'ler, who goes there ?

FREDERICK.

Who questions ?

IVAN.

Daran ! or I do forget
His voice. Daran.

Enter DARAN.

DARAN.

My lord !

IVAN.

        Well ; I have done

Your bidding.

DARAN.

You did right.

IVAN.

        What brings you hither ?

DARAN.

My love for you, my lord—and only that :
The life you serv'd were misbestowed, unless
Devoted to your service, when your good
Required its labours, cares, or sacrifice !
Warn'd by my spies your peace was jeopardis'd,
Touching the cause by the same means informed,—
And further of the remedy advis'd,
I penn'd that scroll, and gave it to the boy.
But what the issue shall be know I not,
Whether it tendeth to thy joy or woe.

IVAN (*Aside to* FREDERICK).

I trust him, Frederick.   He can read my heart ;
Knows it without tuition of my tongue.
What think you of him ?

FREDERICK.

        If the eye and mind
Confess affinity, his thoughts are lit
With knowledge past what school-men boast to teach.

IVAN.

How, Daran, mean you to my joy or woe ?

DARAN.

Woe if you wrong her—woe if you forego her !

IVAN.

How for my weal ?

DARAN.

              Possess her lawfully :
But there your pride demurs.

IVAN.

              You hear him, Frederick.

Reads he my heart ?

DARAN.

              If birth expects her sons
To look so high, pity not make them, too,
Callous of what's below them ; howsoe'er
With beauty, virtue, flourishing, although
No sap it draws from her.

IVAN.

              Frederick, there's learning,
And lofty, too, without the aid of books.
Daran, say on !

DARAN.

              My lord, I am confounded
(No wonder, an unread, untutor'd wight)
With pondering the ways of social men !

Goodness, they say, is all that Heaven regards;
Do they not? They are worshippers of Heav'n;
Are they not? They should love, then, what Heav'n
    loves;
And rate, what Heav'n does, highest; do they so?
A puzzle this, to savage men like me,
Who dwell in woods and wilds.

IVAN.
What mean'st thou, Daran?

DARAN.

Nothing, my lord! What boots it what a rude
Unlettered man can say, who ne'er conn'd book;
Except that common one, which all men ope,
By nature written—plain to mother-wit?
Indeed—indeed, my Lord, a precious thing
To find is love in man or woman.

IVAN.
Yes!
DARAN.

It lasts, my lord, when all beside goes by;
It will work miracles. Life, after all,
Is man's especial good. Through what a rough,
And tedious road he'll drag it. To keep hold,
What will he not let go? It is the chain
That binds him to the fainting galley bench,
And yet he would not snap it. 'Tis the winch
That moves the rack, yet would he have it turn.

But love will give 't away—not risk it—that
Were nothing ! Give it ! Take it to the brink
Of a precipice, and over with 't ; or run it
Right on a rapier's point—nor in the heat
Of doing, but in cool blood—a document
For glory panting in the hosted field
And giving odds to death. Such love, methinks,
Were worth a king's fee ; but the question is,
Hath a king realms to buy it ? Such the love
Borne towards you by the maiden you renounce
Who seeks, for you, a grave, yet flies your bed.

IVAN.

Who seeks for me a grave, yet flies my bed ?
How then, to-morrow, give her to me ?

DARAN.

The parable is true—as I have said,
The end is woe or weal !—which rests with you.

IVAN.

Daran, be plain with him who trusts in thee.
How woe ?

DARAN.

To find a corse in her you love.

IVAN.

How weal ?

DARAN.

To lead her to thy nuptial bed.

A funeral, or bridal, waits for thee—
The maid, a bride or corse—the option thine—
A mourner or a bridegroom !   Now to choose—

IVAN.

Daran, thou sport'st with me.

DARAN (*kneeling*).
Is this to jest ?
My lord, wilt save the maid thou lov'st from death ?
Wilt waive the pride of birth to save her life
This very hour in jeopardy for thine ?

IVAN.

In jeopardy for mine !

DARAN (*rising*).
Thou art betray'd—
Made o'er a bargain to the assassin's knife !
One only way to save thee was descried—
A desperate one—to find a substitute
Would undergo the fate intended thee !
(*Comes close to* IVAN.)
That substitute is found !

IVAN.
In whom ?

DARAN.
The maid
Who once before preserv'd your life, if true
The tale she told, at peril of her own.

IVAN.

Most true the tale.

DARAN.

Whose cherishing of thee
Cost her—what beggars life, if thrown away—
Her virgin love. Whose love, as she affirm'd,
You paid her back (I speak her very words)
With all the glow but not the holiness.

IVAN.

Alas ! most true !

DARAN.

She fled from you—

IVAN.

She did :

DARAN.

To roam the world. Far drearier (she said)
To her than waste where never tree strikes root,
Where never herbage shoots nor water springs !

IVAN.

Oh ! gem, despised, because 'twas poorly set,
Fit for a monarch's crown !

DARAN.

By chance we met.
A lucky chance for me—but what for her ?
An unexpected friend draws out the heart ;

She told me all her story; in return,
The plight you stand in I reveal'd to her.
(*rapidly*) And now—e'en while I tell it you—the blow
That's meant for you her spotless breast awaits!

IVAN.

How? Where? You speak in riddles. Here am I—
Where is the blow? I cannot see it.

DARAN.

No!

But she will feel it—else on me and mine
A curse alight—unless you snatch her from it.

IVAN.

How can I snatch her from it? How?

DARAN.

Unless

The life you save you render worth the care,
What use to her to live?

IVAN (*drawing*).

Slave, to the point,

Or thou shalt die.

DARAN (*Folding his arms*).

Then surely she is dead!

My life, my lord, is yours, of right to take,
Seeing you sav'd it once.

IVAN.

——Daran, speak out!
Ere I would slay thee I would slay myself.
Thy life—my own—the lives of all I love,
I hold as naught, to save that maiden's life.

DARAN.

Then save it, sir.

IVAN.
The way?

DARAN.

There is but one:
But one, by all my hopes!—and I have hopes
More dear to me than the next breath I draw.
One only way.—To plight thy troth to hers.

IVAN.

I'll do it!

FREDERICK.
Ivan!

IVAN.
Yea, though all the world
Said "No!"—I'll do it!

DARAN.
Are you bound to this?

IVAN.
Ay, by my honour—by my honour—all

I reverence—else, the liar's, coward's brand
Stick to me hence—for ever.

DARAN (*wildly*).
>> Then to work.

And would you save her, lose not moment more.
I swear she is in danger—whilst I talked
The precious time was fleeting, and to save
Her heart I fear I've slain her body.   Come!
Ere now the cursed blood-hound's at her throat!

IVAN.

Oh Heaven, protect her!

DARAN.
>> Follow me!

IVAN and FREDERICK.
>> Lead on!
>> *Exeunt hurriedly,* R.

———

SCENE IV.—*Bed room (Set) in the house of* IVAN.
*Time, midnight.   At back, practicable window
opening to the ground; through it is seen the
distant city, and over it the moon.   A couch
is spread with furs and skins.   The usual para-
phernalia of a bed-room scattered about.   Coffers
on table.*

ALEXINA *is discovered sitting in thought on a fauteuil.*

ALEXINA (Rising).

At last the moment comes.   The fate's severe—
Loving and lov'd—and then so soon to die.
But love is the condition of my death.
I am content !   He knew me not again,
Nor pierced the secret of this poor disguise ;
But flushed all eager for the tale should bring
Him back to her—the lost one—who yet stood
Within the beating of his amorous heart.
I am content.   For in his glad confusion,
Beckoning his friend, and straining to be gone,
He marked me not—beyond one passing glance ;—
And so, to glide through corridor and hall,
To try this room and that, and at the last
To attain to this, my tomb, was easy task.

(She walks towards couch.

This couch last night in sleep my lover prest,
And woke at dawn ; the sleep I seek 's eternal.
But still the dread, yet pitying Pow'r that gave
My breath to me—I dare not—do not mock ;
One love is mine on earth, one trust, in Heav'n ;
I live in him—my own poor life is naught.

(She gazes on the moon and stars.

Farewell ! sweet world, with all thy myriad charms,
Farewell ! O moon and stars.   Sad wistful thoughts
Will thrill the heart that parts from youth and life.

(She turns again towards the couch.

Then welcome, death ! grim friend, but still a friend,
Who makest no promise not to be fulfilled,
All misery endeth with thy sharp brief pang,
Thou break'st with endless morn our dreamless sleep.

> (*Shrinks from the couch with horror.*

Yet freezing is his aspect—deep his frown,
His clasp too dread for mortal thoughts to bear,
My soul recoils—life's arms are round me thrown—
Away ! Such dalliance is not for me.

(*She unclasps her collar and prepares to lie down on
couch.*

O spirits, ministers of Heaven's high will,
Be near to aid me in this awful hour !

> (*She rests on the couch previous to lying down.*

My fears are past ; and now for sleep serene !
The death in life—the life in death. (*Pause.*) Farewell !

She reclines on couch. Pause. ROBERT *and* CATHERINE
appear behind at window cloaked. CATHERINE *bears
dark lanthorn and* ROBERT *a poignard. They enter
softly by window and grope down stage.*

ROBERT.

Hush, wife ! tread lightly as the summer air
When the aspen leaf is still ! Unveil the light
Slow as a dubious dawn.

> *She withdraws the shade a little.*

Is this his room ?

Look for the signs !

CATHERINE (*Turning light on wall*).
That is his portrait, sure,
And these his coffers.   (*Touches them.*)

ROBERT (*Clutching at them*).
Ha ! I know them well—
And the bed—(*She discovers it*) 'tis he !

CATHERINE (*Approaching.*)
He sleeps—

ROBERT (*Feeling his dagger*).
Ay ! ne'er to wake.

Distant bells chime the hour. ROBERT, *who has ap-
proached the bed, starts back.*

ROBERT.

Stay ! Hist !

CATHERINE.
What now?   Art terrified ?

ROBERT.
No—no !

But heard you nought ?

CATHERINE.
A distant bell—that's all.

ROBERT.

One moment—something seems to hold my hand.

CATHERINE.

Remember! Coward!

ROBERT.

I do! and so away
With scruple! He but dreams he hates his foe
Who hesitates to kill! I'll do it now!

ROBERT *approaches his victim. Hesitates. At last
lifts his knife to strike, when the door is burst open
and enter* IVAN, DARAN, *and* FREDERICK. CATHE-
RINE *shrieks.* IVAN *thrusts at* ROBERT, *who has
turned in terror from the couch. He falls.* ALEXINA
springs from bed, and clasping her arms round
IVAN, *falls on his breast.*

ALEXINA (*In broken utterances*).

Saved! Doubly saved!

IVAN.

My love! my love!

DARAN (*Going towards window, and stretching his
right arm solemnly towards* IVAN).

Thy oath

Remember!

>(*Long pause.* IVAN *mutely attests his faith.*
>
>She was true—TRUE UNTO DEATH!

(*Tableau.* C. IVAN *and* ALEXINA. *In front of them lies* ROBERT, *with* CATHERINE *kneeling beside him.* L. FREDERICK. *Behind, with his hand still raised and half turned to go,* DARAN.

CURTAIN.

Printed at the Regent Press, 55, King Street, Regent Street, W.